ON LINE

NONSENSE!
HE YELLED

BY
ROGER ESCHBACHER

PICTURES BY
ADRIAN JOHNSON

Dial Books for Young Readers

NEW YORK

Published by
Dial Books for Young Readers
A division of Penguin Putnam Inc.
345 Hudson Street · New York, New York 10014

— · — · — · — · — · —

Text copyright © 2002 by Roger Eschbacher
Pictures copyright © 2002 by Adrian Johnson
All rights reserved
Designed by Nancy R. Leo-Kelly
Printed in Hong Kong on acid-free paper
1 3 5 7 9 10 8 6 4 2

Library of Congress Cataloging-in-Publication Data
Eschbacher, Roger.
Nonsense! he yelled / by Roger Eschbacher ;
pictures by Adrian Johnson.
p.   cm.
Summary: Twenty-five unusual boys and one girl
describe themselves in short humorous verses.
ISBN 0-8037-2582-5
[1. Nonsense verses. 2. Stories in rhyme.]
I. Johnson, Adrian, ill. II. Title.
PZ8.3.E84 No 2002   [E]—dc21   00-024077

— · — · — · — · — · —

The art was created from ink line drawings,
which were scanned and completed using
Adobe Photoshop and Adobe Illustrator.

— · — · — · — · — · —

To Margie, Molly, Erin, and Claire,
who keep my life filled with love, fun,
and nonsense R.E.

For Rachel Elizabeth Sugarbutty Johnson A.J.

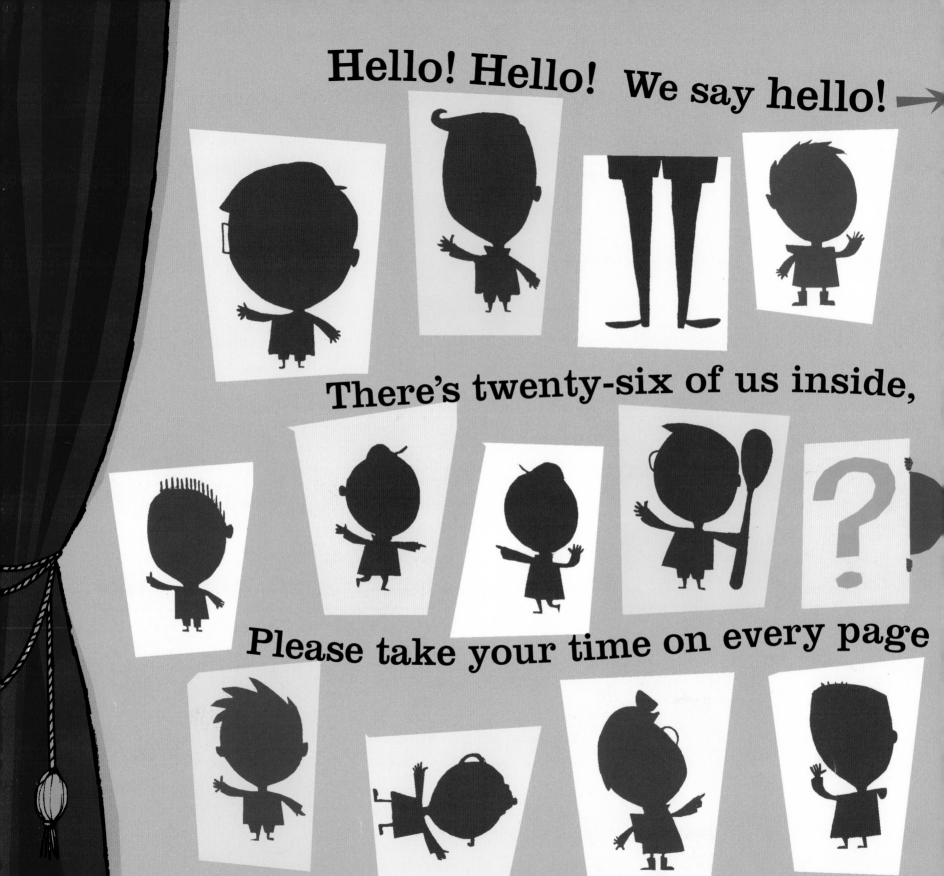

Hello! Hello! We say hello!

There's twenty-six of us inside,

Please take your time on every page

There's boys in here of every age,

We're mighty glad to greet you.

and each would like to meet you.

so that you get to know us.

with nonsense words below us!

My name is Bob, I hold a knob.
I did not ask to have this job.
I found it on the floor one day,
And now I can't give it away.

My name is Dean,
I grew one bean.
It's red and yellow,
blue and green!
My rainbow bean is odd,
that's true—
I bet that Gene
will like it too!

My name is Ed
And I am red.

I wish that I
were blue instead.

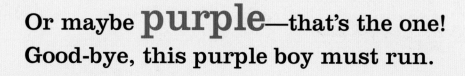

Or maybe purple—that's the one!
Good-bye, this purple boy must run.

CRANK

My name is Frank, I drive a tank,
The kind of tank that you must crank.
I wind it up and jump inside,
Then take it for a bumpy ride.

My name is Gene,
I'm feeling mean—
And that's because
of Dean's odd bean.
I stuck it in
a pot of mine
And now my house
sits on a vine.

HANK'S TANK

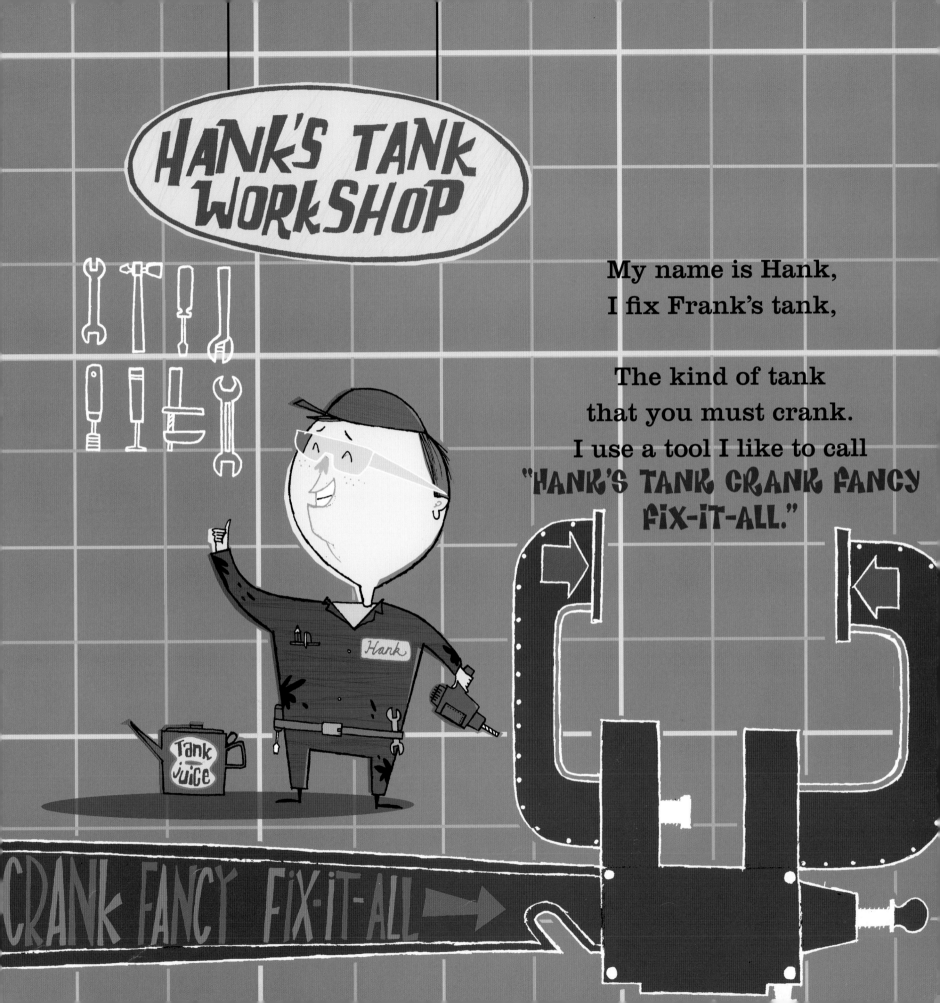

My name is Irv, And I've got nerve. I'll race my bike down any curve. I ride so fast that things get **blurry**. My friends all say, " Irv

NO SPEEDING

520mph

My name is Jake,
I stay awake
From dusk, all night,
until daybreak.
I lay in bed
but I'm not sleepy.
Those monsters on TV
are CREEPY!

what's the hurry?"

My name is Lyle.
My brother Kyle
Is running from that crocodile.
Kyle's fast enough to be the winner,
So now that croc wants *ME* for dinner!

My name is Kyle.
This crocodile
Has climbed out of the river Nile.
He claims he did so just to meet me,
But I suspect he'd rather eat me.

My name is Moss,
I'm at a loss.
I found three **tons**
of applesauce.
Should I put it
on a shelf?
Or try and eat it
all myself?

My name is Nell.
As you can tell,
This book of boys
has me as well.
Yes, I'm a girl,
I'm glad to say.
So should I go?
NO! I will stay.

My name is Og,
And I'm a Trog,
A caveboy who lives near a bog.
It's wet and smells,
but that's okay—
A bog Trog likes to
live that way.

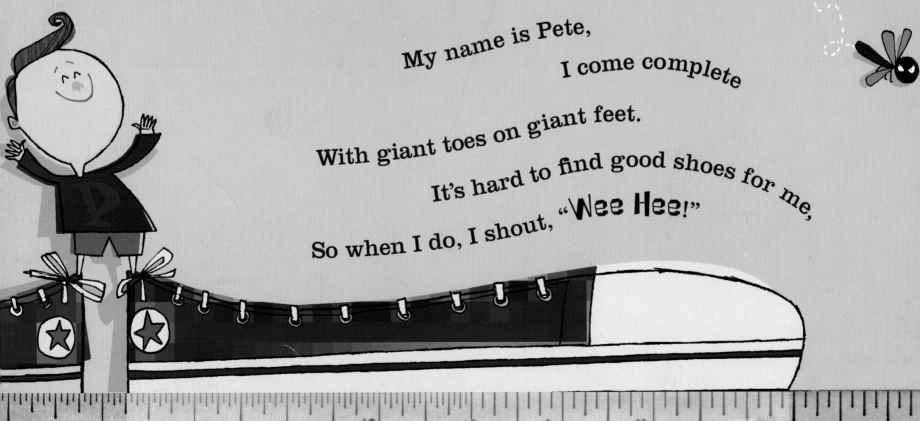

My name is Pete,
I come complete
With giant toes on giant feet.
It's hard to find good shoes for me,
So when I do, I shout, "Wee Hee!"

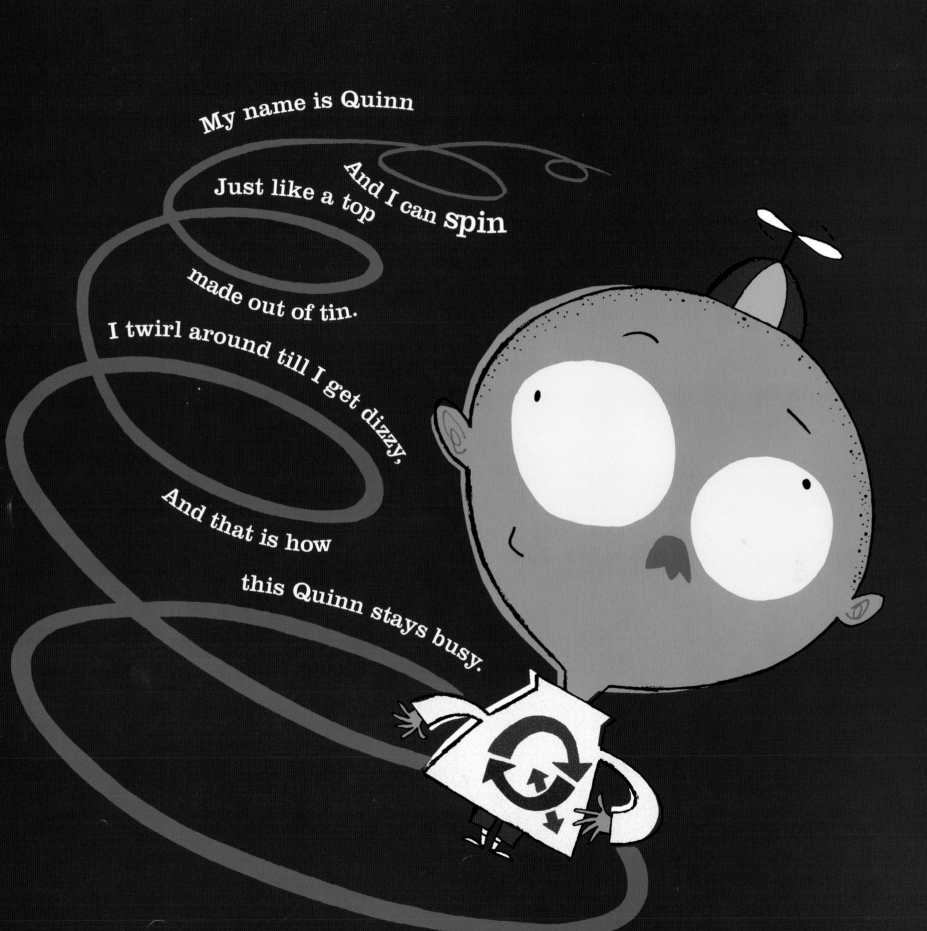

My name is Quinn

And I can spin

Just like a top

made out of tin.

I twirl around till I get dizzy,

And that is how

this Quinn stays busy.

My name is Reed,
I own a steed
That won't eat hay, it eats birdseed.
It sits up in a tree and sings,
And flaps its hooves around
like wings.

My name is Ty

The Human Fly.

The **tallest**
buildings
catch
my eye.
I like to
climb
up to
the top,
But
going
down
is
quite
a
DROP!

My name is **Uz**.
Here's what **Uz** does:
I look around till I find **fuzz**.
I scoop it up into my bag,
Then mark each with
an **Uz** bag tag.

My name is Vern
And my concern
Is where to put my potted fern.
Should I put it on my bed?

Or on my sister's HEAD instead?

My name is Wade
And in the **shade**
I like to sell my lemonade.
'Cause when it's HOT
and way too sunny,
A kid like me
can make good money!

My name is
Xerk, I'm paid
to lurk—

You see, I do
detective work.

I love to sneak and skulk about.

It's lurk-while-work

without a

doubt.

My name is Yat

From planet Zat,

Where everyone

acts like a cat.

PLANET ZOG

We stay away from
planet Zog,
Where everyone
acts like a dog.

My name is Zack,
It's hair I lack.

I'm quite bald from front to back.
My head is SHINY, that's for sure,
But I am proud, I want no cure.

front   BACK

goyette's
HEAD POLISH

Shampoo

----

is my name
And I can claim
I'm in this strange book's
HALL OF FAME.
I'm proud of this,
that is for certain.
Good-bye! Good-bye!
Let's draw the curtain!